For Jaime
and the beautiful shining silence
—— & ——
For Donna McCarthy
who'll always be a part of the team

A

First published in Great Britain in 2018 by Andersen Press Ltd.,
20 Vauxhall Bridge Road, London SW1V 2SA.
Published by special arrangement with Clarion Books,
an imprint of Houghton Mifflin Harcourt Publishing Company,
and Rights People, London.

Text and illustrations copyright © 2018 by David Wiesner.

1 3 5 7 9 10 8 6 4 2

British Library Cataloguing in Publication Data available.
ISBN 978 1 78344 742 8

I GOT IT!

David Wiesner

ANDERSEN PRESS

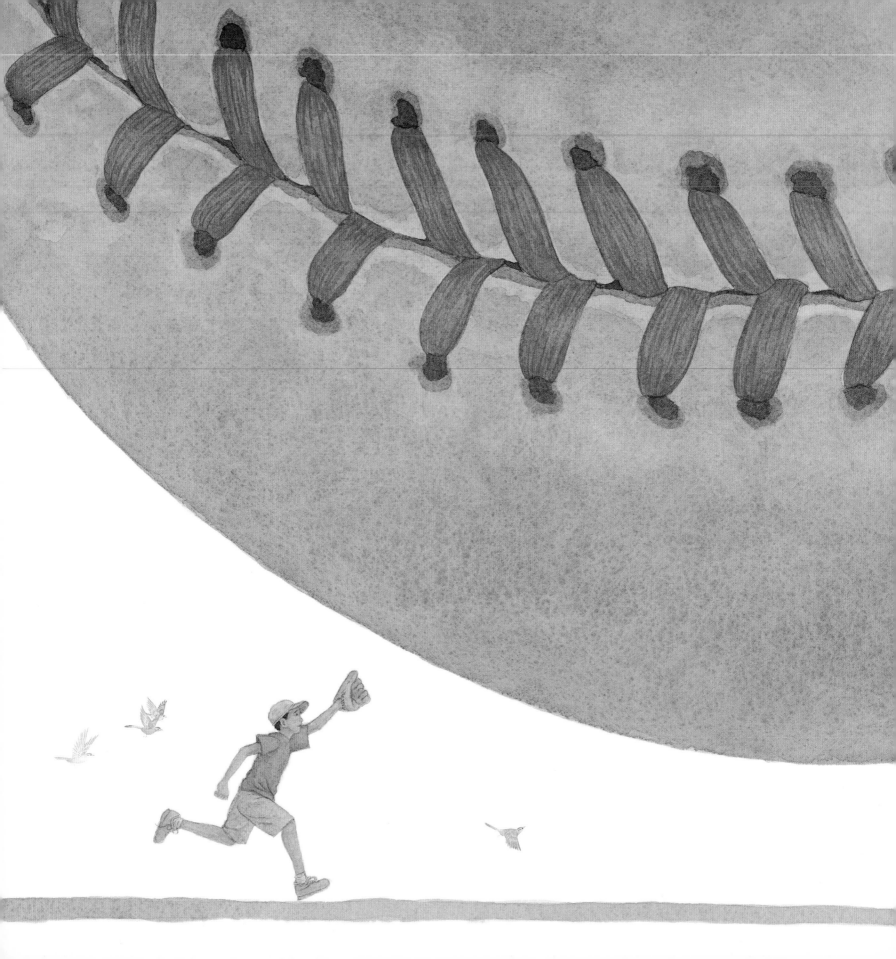

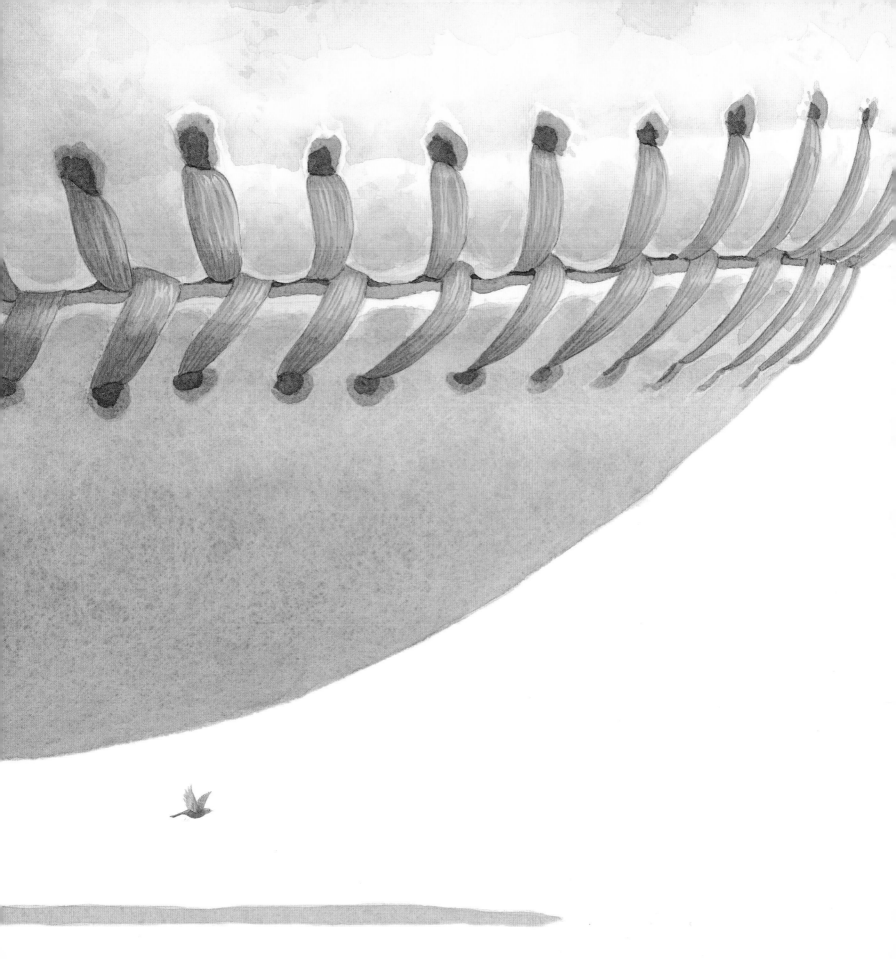